Whispered Secrets of the Jade Physician

Jasmine Lee

Published by Jasmine Lee, 2023.

Introduction

"Whispered Secrets of the Jade Physician" delves into the heart-wrenching journey of Wu Jian, a renowned healer yearning for the affection of his devoted disciple, Li Mingyi. As their relationship unfolds amidst a backdrop of ancient customs and societal expectations, Wu Jian must navigate the delicate balance between professional duty and personal desires. This captivating novel takes readers on an emotional rollercoaster, exploring the complexities of love, loyalty, and the sacrifices one must make in the pursuit of true happiness. Prepare to be swept away by a tale of passion, longing, and the boundless depths of the human heart.

When will the bright moon appear? With a cup of wine, I ask the blue sky.
I know not in which heavenly palace, tonight is of what year.
I long to ride the wind and return, but I fear the jade palaces and ivory towers are too cold.
So I rise and dance with my own shadow, how could it compare to being in the mortal world?
Turning the crimson hall, leaning on the embroidered screen, the reflection accompanies my sleepless night.
There should be no resentment, why does the full moon turn to a crescent when we part?
People experience joy and sorrow, parting and reunions, and the moon waxes and wanes,
These things have been so since ancient times, impossible to be complete.
I only wish people could live long, and share the beauty of the moon even if we are thousands of miles apart.

—————— **Li Bai**

Contents:

Characters:

Wu Jian - the Jade Physician, whose heart is captivated by Li Mingyi.

Zihua / Li Mingyi - Wu Jian's dedicated disciple.

Lin Xia - a jealous girl from Qingmei, who holds unrequited love towards Wu Jian.

Li Cheng - Li Mingyi's older brother.

Li Xuan - Li Mingyi's younger brother.

Lady Li - Li Mingyi's mother, an elegant and influential woman.

Li Guang - Li Mingyi's father.

Zhang Xiangyu - Li Mingyi's suitor from a noble family.

Liang Xue - a girl in love with Zhang Xiangyu.

Cheng Ming - a merchant, Wu Jian's friend.

Chapter 1: "The Serene Footsteps of the Jade Physician"

The sun cast its golden rays upon the sprawling village of Qingmei, nestled in the lush valleys of ancient China. Amidst the bustling streets, a figure emerged, captivating the attention of onlookers with an air of mystery and purpose. Wu Jian, the village's revered physician, walked with measured steps, his presence commanding respect and admiration.

Tall and lean, Wu Jian possessed an aura that drew others towards him, their eyes entranced by the enigmatic depths of his piercing gaze. Clad in flowing robes of indigo silk, his attire mirrored the serene elegance of the surrounding landscapes.

Wu Jian's reputation as a healer extended far beyond Qingmei's borders. His knowledge of medicinal herbs and ancient healing techniques surpassed that of his peers, earning him the title of the "Jade Physician." From common ailments to life-threatening diseases, he possessed the power to alleviate suffering and restore hope where it seemed lost.

As he navigated the streets, a soft smile played upon Wu Jian's lips, born of the genuine satisfaction that came from his life's purpose: the alleviation of human suffering. The villagers regarded him as a guardian, an embodiment of their hopes and dreams. They sought solace in his words, in the gentle touch of his healing hands.

Yet, behind the compassionate façade, Wu Jian carried the weight of his own personal battles. His eyes bore witness to the fragility of life, and within the depths of his heart, a longing stirred. For all his wisdom and expertise, he remained haunted by a profound loneliness that lingered like a shadow, reminding him of the sacrifices he had made for his craft.

As the sun began its descent, casting an amber glow over the village, Wu Jian knew that his destiny beckoned him beyond the borders of Qingmei. Little did he anticipate that his path would soon intersect with another, a woman whose presence would ignite a flame within him, both captivating and perilous.

As the moon cast its silvery glow over the village of Qingmei, Wu Jian, the Jade Physician, found himself consumed by a restless anticipation. The upcoming dawn held the promise of a new day, and he knew it was time to replenish his medicinal supplies with the treasures of the forest.

With the first light of dawn, Wu Jian rose from his humble bed, his mind already buzzing with the tasks that lay ahead. The morning mist enveloped the village, painting an ethereal backdrop for his journey into the woods. It was in the early hours, when the world was still cloaked in slumber, that the forest revealed its most potent secrets.

Equipped with a woven basket and his trusted walking stick, Wu Jian set forth with a quiet determination. Each step carried him closer to the heart of the woodland sanctuary, his senses heightened, attuned to the symphony of nature's awakening.

As he ventured deeper into the forest, the fragrance of dew-kissed leaves and earth permeated the air. The rustling of creatures and the melodious songs of birds became his companions on this solitary pilgrimage. Wu Jian's keen eyes scanned the verdant landscape, seeking the telltale signs of rare herbs and medicinal plants.

With practiced grace, he plucked delicate petals and carefully uprooted healing roots, always mindful of maintaining the delicate balance of nature's bounty. Every herb he gathered was a lifeline, a source of relief and rejuvenation for those entrusted to his care.

Time seemed to stand still in the tranquil embrace of the forest, as Wu Jian's basket filled with the treasures of the woodland realm. A sense of satisfaction warmed his heart, for he knew that with each herb collected, he was one step closer to alleviating the suffering of his patients.

As he emerged from the forest, the rising sun greeted him with its golden rays, casting a radiant glow upon his weary but contented face. The morning's endeavor had not only replenished his stock of medicinal herbs, but it had also rekindled his spirit, infusing him with a renewed sense of purpose.

With his basket brimming with nature's healing gifts, Wu Jian returned to Qingmei, ready to bring solace and hope to those in need. The forest had once again offered its silent guidance, and Wu Jian, the Jade Physician, was grateful for the privilege of being its humble messenger.

Lost in the tranquility of his forest expedition, Wu Jian's acute senses detected an unfamiliar disturbance in the symphony of nature. A rustle of leaves and a muffled cry caught his attention, drawing him towards an unexpected encounter. As he approached, his eyes widened in awe and disbelief.

Chapter 2: "The Enchanted Encounter"

Amidst the dappled sunlight filtering through the canopy, lay an injured figure—an ethereal vision of unearthly beauty. Wu Jian couldn't help but be captivated by her delicate features and the grace with which she carried herself. Time seemed to stand still as he beheld the enchanting sight before him.

Composing himself, Wu Jian focused on the urgency of the situation. Kneeling beside the wounded young lady, he saw blood staining her flowing garments, her face reflecting both pain and vulnerability. With a tender touch, he assessed her injuries, his hands moving with the precision of a healer honed by years of practice.

Drawing upon his collection of medicinal herbs, Wu Jian carefully administered remedies to ease her pain and aid in the healing process. His heart swelled with compassion, as he sensed an unspoken connection between them, transcending the bounds of mere chance.

At that moment, Wu Jian recognized that their meeting was no ordinary occurrence. The forest had conspired to bring them together, intertwining their destinies in a tapestry woven with threads of healing, beauty, and an inexplicable bond.

Concern etched upon Wu Jian's face. "Forgive me, miss. Are you alright? What is your name? How did you get here?" he inquired softly, his voice carrying a hint of gentleness.

She looked at him, her eyes reflecting a mixture of confusion and gratitude. "I... I do not remember," she whispered, her voice delicate as a whispering breeze.

Wu Jian's brows furrowed with empathy. "You have no recollection of how you came to be here?"

She shook her head, her expression filled with a tinge of sadness. "I do not remember anything..."

Wu Jian's compassion deepened as he knelt beside her, his voice soothing. "Fear not, for you are safe now.

A flicker of trust and relief illuminated her eyes as she looked at Wu Jian, finding solace in his presence. "Thank you," she murmured, her voice resonating with a mix of gratitude and vulnerability. "I am grateful for your kindness."

Together, they sat in the serene forest, Wu Jian attending to her wounds with delicate care. They spoke little, their silence filled with a shared understanding that transcended words. As he tended to her, he couldn't help but feel a connection—an inexplicable bond that defied explanation but felt undeniably real.

As their encounter in the forest drew to a close, Wu Jian extended a heartfelt offer. "If you have nowhere else to go, I welcome you to my humble abode," he gently proposed. A glimmer of appreciation sparked in her eyes as she accepted his invitation.

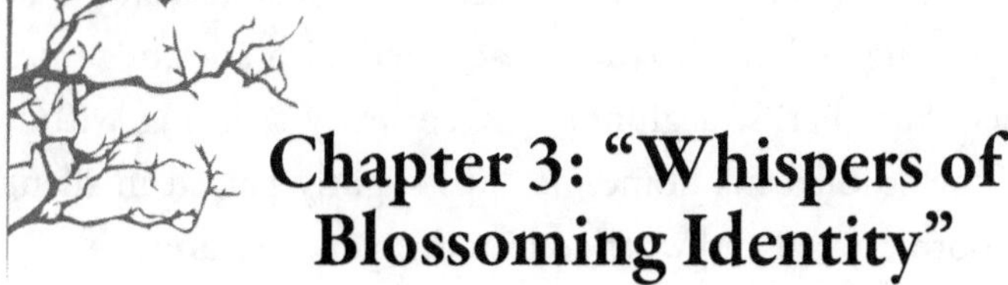

Chapter 3: "Whispers of Blossoming Identity"

Wu Jian's home nestled amidst the embrace of nature's bounty, a sanctuary of tranquility that beckoned weary souls. As they stepped through the door, a sense of serenity washed over them, as if the walls themselves whispered tales of solace and healing.

Soft, diffused light filtered through gossamer curtains, casting a gentle glow on the worn wooden floors. The air carried the delicate fragrance of medicinal herbs, a testament to Wu Jian's devotion to his craft. Artful scrolls adorned the walls, depicting the graceful sweep of landscapes and the intricate beauty of blooming flora.

A modest hearth crackled in the heart of the home, casting a warm glow that illuminated the nooks and crannies. Comfortable seating arrangements invited respite and reflection. Shelves lined with weathered books and jars brimming with herbal remedies stood as testaments to Wu Jian's accumulated wisdom and unwavering passion.

Woven rugs, crafted with care, adorned the floor, offering a touch of comfort and grounding. Windows framed breathtaking views of the surrounding lush greenery, inviting the splendor of nature inside.

Within these humble walls, Wu Jian's home embodied the essence of compassion and healing. It was a space where weariness found solace, where troubled hearts found respite, and where the gentle touch of his skilled hands and kind words worked miracles. In this nurturing haven, their intertwined journeys would unfold, and the power of empathy and human connection would flourish.

With each passing moment, Wu Jian observed her keen gaze sweep across his humble abode, taking in every detail as if committing it to memory. Her eyes lingered on the shelves adorned with ancient tomes and vials of medicinal herbs, a glimmer of curiosity sparking within them. The way she studied his home, her lips slightly parted in silent contemplation, both excited and worried him in equal measure.

He couldn't help but wonder what thoughts danced through her mind. What secrets did she unearth in the confines of his dwelling? The unknown reason for his simultaneous excitement and unease remained elusive, tucked away in the recesses of his subconscious.

Within the serene confines of Wu Jian's home, her gaze held a hint of curiosity and compassion. "May I ask, what is your name?" she inquired, her voice soft and gentle.

A flicker of melancholy passed through Wu Jian's eyes as he met her gaze. "I am Wu Jian," he replied, his voice carrying a touch of wistfulness. "As for living arrangements, I have dwelled here alone since my parents passed away several years ago."

Her expression softened, understanding the weight of his loss and the echoes of longing it left behind.

As they stood within the soothing sanctuary of Wu Jian's home, a question stirred within him, tender and filled with genuine curiosity. "Do you remember how old you are? Who are your parents?" he asked, his voice gentle and warm.

A melancholic shadow passed over her delicate features, and a hint of sadness tinged her eyes. "I... I don't remember," she murmured softly, her voice tinged with both frustration and a touch of vulnerability.

An empathetic ache surged through Wu Jian's being, his heart both sorrowful and hopeful. In the midst of her amnesia, he saw an opportunity, a chance for her to find solace and belonging in his embrace, unburdened by the shackles of her former self.

A delicate smile touched his lips, brimming with compassion. If she did not remember who she was, then perhaps she could find a new beginning within the sanctuary of his home. In that moment, a glimmer of hope illuminated his heart, whispering that their intertwined destinies were meant to unfold in this unforeseen twist of fate.

As the sun dipped below the horizon, Wu Jian's eyes shimmered with purpose. "Then I will call you Zihua," he declared. "Zihua, the lavender blossom, capturing the delicate essence of the flower I discovered just before finding you."

Wu Jian watched Zihua's face light up with joy and gratitude. "Thank you, Wu Jian," she murmured, her voice filled with appreciation. "The name you've given me, Zihua, it's truly beautiful."

Wu Jian hesitantly offered, "Zihua, please, rest upon the bed. It's more comfortable for you." But Zihua shook her head, refusing the generous offer. Determined, Wu Jian insisted, "I'll be fine on the floor."

Chapter 4: "The Guiding Flames of Mentorship"

For the entirety of the week that followed, Wu Jian devoted himself to Zihua's care. With unwavering dedication, he ensured her comfort, tending to her needs and offering her nourishing meals and herbal concoctions. He patiently answered her countless questions, sharing stories and knowledge of the healing arts. Wu Jian's gentle presence became her guiding light, providing solace in the face of her lost memories. Every day, he watched over her, offering a steady hand and a warm smile.

As Zihua delved into the intricate world of medicine under Wu Jian's guidance, her innate intelligence shone brilliantly. With a voracious thirst for knowledge, she absorbed each lesson with a remarkable acumen. Her sharp observations and insightful questions amazed Wu Jian, and he marveled at her innate understanding of the healing arts. Zihua's intellectual prowess combined with her deep empathy made her a remarkable student, leaving Wu Jian in awe of her natural talents and the untapped potential hidden within her.

Word of a mysterious lady residing with Wu Jian soon spread through the village, fueling the fires of curiosity and gossip. Whispers floated in the air, weaving tales of forbidden love and scandalous affairs. The villagers couldn't resist speculating about the nature of their relationship, their tongues wagging with innuendos and assumptions.

In an unfortunate twist, Zihua caught wind of the village's gossip. Whispers of their unconventional arrangement reached her ears, stirring a mix of emotions within her.

Zihua's heart brimmed with gratitude for Wu Jian, but a profound fear of jeopardizing his esteemed reputation consumed her thoughts. Determined to honor their bond, she resolved to approach him, requesting to be taken in as his disciple. She understood the significance of the teacher-student relationship, akin to a father's guidance, and believed it would provide a safe haven where their connection could flourish without the weight of societal judgments.

Zihua entered their tranquil sanctuary, her heart brimming with gratitude and determination. Approaching Wu Jian, who was engrossed in his studies, she gathered her courage.

Zihua: "Wu Jian, I want to express my deepest gratitude for your kindness and guidance. I am truly blessed to have found you. I have thought long and hard, and I wish to ask you to take me as your disciple. I want to learn from you and assist you in any way I can. I can take care of the household chores and support you in your work."

As Zihua expressed her gratitude and determination, Wu Jian's heart clenched with a mix of emotions. In her words, he discerned a genuine admiration and appreciation, but an undeniable pang of sadness washed over him as he realized she did not perceive him as a man.

A wave of self-doubt crashed upon his thoughts, wondering if his age or appearance played a role in her perception. Despite his youthful, handsome features, he questioned if he fell short of the captivating allure that would stir romantic sentiments within her.

With a heavy sigh, he silently accepted the painful truth. Their connection, at least in her eyes, seemed confined to a teacher-student dynamic. The wounded ache in his heart mingled with a profound longing, as he quietly resolved to preserve their bond and cherish the gratitude she expressed, even if it meant stifling his own unrequited feelings.

Wu Jian: "Zihua, your offer touches my heart. Your dedication and willingness to support me are admirable. If you are willing to take on such responsibilities, then I gladly accept you as my disciple. Together, we will navigate the path of medicine."

Their days unfolded in a harmonious rhythm, bound by their shared pursuit of healing. Wu Jian and Zihua embarked on a journey together, venturing to Wu Jian's private practice to tend to the ailments of the villagers.

With each passing day, their bond grew stronger, complemented by their individual skills. Wu Jian, with his profound knowledge and experience, guided Zihua in the art of medicine, while she, with her innate talent and unwavering determination, absorbed his teachings with remarkable grace.

As they ventured through the village, their presence brought solace to those in need. They worked tirelessly, employing their skills and offering remedies with compassion, witnessing the transformative power of their combined efforts.

In the midst of their healing endeavors, Wu Jian and Zihua discovered a profound joy in each other's company. The tender moments shared amidst their work brought warmth to their hearts, nurturing a deep affection that lingered just beneath the surface.

In the tranquil moments between their healing endeavors, Wu Jian found solace in simply being by Zihua's side. The thought of spending his days in her presence, even without reciprocated love, filled him with a quiet contentment. For him, the prospect of a lifetime shared together brought a profound sense of happiness.

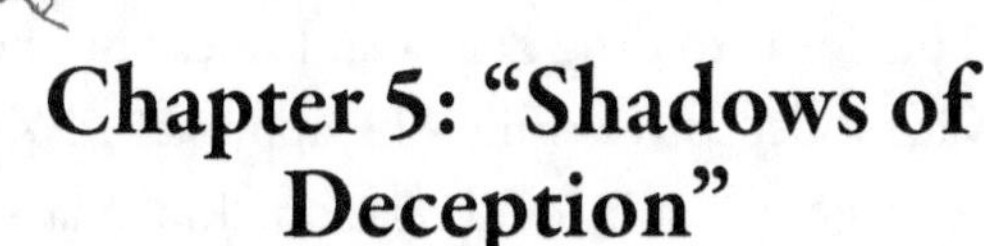

Chapter 5: "Shadows of Deception"

Lin Xia was raised in a world of indulgence and privilege, spoiled by her affluent family. Her appearance, though unremarkable, did little to hinder her entitled attitude. Rather than kindness, she exuded an air of self-importance, fueled by her belief that she deserved special treatment due to her status and upbringing.

As the village buzzed with whispers of Wu Jian's new disciple, Lin Xia returned from her visit to the city, her heart heavy with conflicting emotions. Since childhood, she had secretly harbored deep affection for Wu Jian, but now, the news of his new protégé sent a surge of jealousy and resentment coursing through her veins.

Confronting him, Lin Xia's voice trembled with hurt and frustration. "Wu Jian, how could you take in a female disciple without considering my feelings? Have you forgotten our history, the bond we once shared?"

Wu Jian's gaze remained cold, his voice devoid of warmth. "Lin Xia, the path I've chosen does not revolve around personal feelings."

Her heart shattered as his dismissive words hit her like shards of ice. With a bitter sigh, Lin Xia turned away, realizing that her unrequited love had been met with indifference.

As Lin Xia witnessed Wu Jian's attention being drawn towards Zihua, a bitter determination took hold of her heart. Fueled by jealousy, she vowed to win over Wu Jian's affections, even if it meant resorting to dark emotions. Hatred seeped into her thoughts, poisoning her perception of Zihua, who had unknowingly become her rival.

With each passing day, Lin Xia's plan solidified. She would manipulate situations, casting doubts and sowing discord, all in the name of winning Wu Jian's heart.

Her devious plan was to drug Zihua and smear her honor with her cousin's help. With a deceptive smile, she approached Zihua, feigning friendship and engaging her in conversation. Lin Xia suggested that Zihua visit her aunt's house, claiming her aunt felt sick. Zihua, ever kind hearted, agreed to visit Lin Xia's aunt's house.

As Wu Jian noticed Zihua's absence from his private practice, a sense of unease washed over him. She always told him where she was planning to go and her not doing it this time raised his suspicions, especially with Lin Xia lurking nearby.

Wu Jian paced anxiously, his eyes darting between Lin Xia and the empty space where Zihua should have been. "Where is Zihua?" he demanded, his voice laced with concern.

A sly smile curled on Lin Xia's lips. "Oh, Wu Jian, you're just in time," she teased, trying to deflect his question. "I have something fascinating to show you. If you'll just wait a little longer..."

Impatience tinged Wu Jian's voice. "No more games, Lin Xia. Tell me, where is Zihua?"

Lin Xia's expression hardened, her eyes narrowing. "Why are you so worried about her?" she retorted, her voice laced with venom. "Maybe she doesn't want to be with you anymore."

Wu Jian's heart skipped a beat, his eyes widening in disbelief. "What are you implying?"

With a calculated pause, Lin Xia smirked. "Oh, nothing... Just that Zihua might be enjoying herself elsewhere. You should have kept a closer eye on her."

Dread washed over Wu Jian, fueling his determination. "Tell me where she is, Lin Xia. Now!" he demanded, his voice firm and resolute, unwilling to let her manipulations sway him.

Lin Xia hesitated, then begrudgingly replied, "Fine, she's at my aunt's house."

Hurrying through the streets, Wu Jian's heart raced with concern for Zihua. Arriving at Lin Xia's aunt's house, he discovered Zihua standing over Lin Xia's unconscious cousin, her expression a mix of vigilance and concern.

"What happened here?" Wu Jian inquired, his voice filled with worry.

Zihua turned to face him, her eyes flashing with determination. "Shifu! I sensed something amiss with Lin Xia's cousin. He attempted to take advantage of the situation but I intervened, neutralizing his intentions and ensuring his safety."

Wu Jian's eyes widened, a mix of shock and anger coursing through him. "Lin Xia's cousin... he planned to harm you?"

Zihua nodded. "It appears so. Do not worry, shifu. I am unharmed, and I will protect myself."

A profound sense of admiration and gratitude washed over Wu Jian as he realized the extent of Zihua's skill and dedication. She had not only learned the art of healing but had also embraced the virtues of respect and loyalty. He was filled with renewed pride in his disciple.

Overwhelmed by a surge of emotions, Wu Jian couldn't restrain himself any longer. He pulled Zihua into a heartfelt embrace, silently conveying his gratitude, pride, and affection. Determined to support her, he vowed to confront Lin Xia and put an end to her malicious schemes.

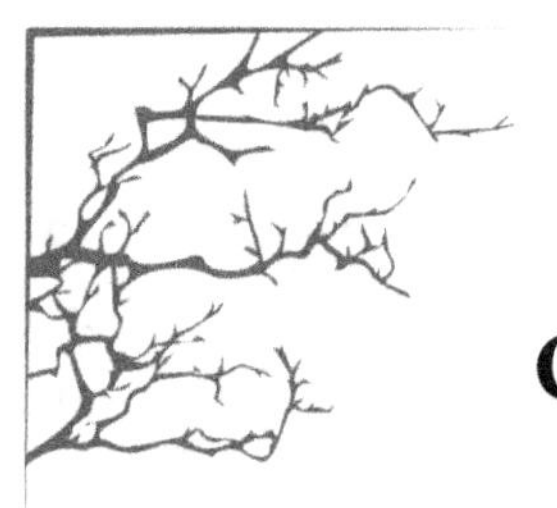

Chapter 6: "The Reckoning"

Kindness flows naturally within Wu Jian's being, radiating from his very core. His compassionate nature guides his every action and decision. Whether it's caring for the sick, offering solace to the troubled, or lending a helping hand to those in need, Wu Jian's innate kindness knows no bounds. His gentle words and warm smile bring comfort and reassurance to those around him. Even in the face of adversity, he finds a way to extend a hand of compassion and understanding. Wu Jian's kindness is not a mere act, but an integral part of his character that shapes his interactions with others, fostering a sense of love, acceptance, and healing. His genuine care for people touches hearts and inspires others to embrace kindness in their own lives.

Conflicts were an arena Wu Jian deemed beneath his dignified presence. He recognized the futility of engaging in petty disputes and trivial arguments. Instead, he chose the path of peace and harmony, finding solace in resolving conflicts through compassion and understanding. Wu Jian's serene demeanor and wisdom allowed him to navigate through tense situations with grace and poise. He understood that true strength lay not in dominating others but in fostering unity and cooperation. His aversion to conflicts was not out of weakness, but a testament to his elevated character and enlightened perspective. Wu Jian believed in the power of empathy and believed that by leading through example, he could inspire others to seek resolutions through peaceful means.

This time, however, was an exception to Wu Jian's usual calm and composed demeanor. For the first time in his life, he was consumed by an overwhelming fury that surged through his veins. The mere thought of someone attempting to harm his beloved Zihua ignited a fire within him, fueling his determination to take action. His anger, normally dormant, transformed him into a force to be reckoned with. Wu Jian's usually serene countenance was replaced by a steely resolve as he vowed to put an end to the malicious schemes and protect Zihua at all costs. This fierce protectiveness awakened a side of him he had never known, propelling him to lengths he never thought possible. Love had unleashed a dormant rage within him, making it clear that when it came to safeguarding those he cherished, Wu Jian would stop at nothing.

With a mischievous glint in his eyes, Wu Jian hatched a clever plan to teach Lin Xia a lesson she would never forget. Expertly forging her handwriting, he composed a heartfelt love letter in her name and dispatched it to the village's notorious bully, renowned for his penchant for brothels and scandalous affairs. Wu Jian knew that the contents of the letter would rouse the bully's curiosity and stir up chaos in Lin Xia's reputation. As the love letter found its way into the hands of its unsuspecting recipient, Wu Jian observed from a distance, eagerly awaiting the fallout. It was an audacious move, a playful twist of fate that would expose Lin Xia's true colors and make her reconsider the consequences of her malicious schemes.

In the depths of Wu Jian's mischievous plan, a pang of unease tugged at his heart. He couldn't bear the thought of Zihua discovering his devious act and thinking less of him. Deep down, he knew that Zihua held purity and kindness in her heart, and he wanted to protect that image. So, he kept his secret hidden, deciding not to disclose the truth to her. It was a burden he would bear alone, for he believed that the ends justified the means in this particular instance. Wu Jian hoped that, in due time, Lin Xia would learn her lesson and mend her ways, sparing Zihua from any further harm.

As fate would have it, Lin Xia's world was turned upside down by the consequences of Wu Jian's cunning plan. The love letter, supposedly penned by her, found its way into the hands of the village's notorious bully. Rumors spread like wildfire, tarnishing Lin Xia's reputation and subjecting her to scorn and ridicule. She suffered the consequences of her own deceit, unaware that Wu Jian had orchestrated it all.

Chapter 7: "The Dance of Steel and Heart"

Zihua possessed a cascade of lustrous ebony hair that flowed down her back, accentuating her graceful demeanor. Her hair, meticulously arranged in a simple yet elegant style, framed her face with a touch of natural beauty. Adorned in flowing garments, she radiated a sense of tranquility and gracefulness.

Her eyes, like pools of deep and thoughtful obsidian, held an aura of wisdom and empathy. They sparkled with a gentle curiosity and a hint of mischief, revealing a playful spirit hidden within. Her hands, slender and nimble, showed the delicate balance of strength and grace. They were the instruments through which she applied her healing touch and displayed her dedication to the practice of medicine.

Zihua's overall appearance reflected a harmonious blend of inner serenity and outward poise. She carried herself with a quiet confidence, captivating those around her with her gentle presence and the undeniable aura of compassion that emanated from within.

Zihua couldn't help but notice the way Wu Jian's eyes lingered on her. At first, she attributed it to their close friendship, mistaking it for a warm and friendly gaze. However, as she observed him more closely, she detected a subtle intensity in his eyes—a glimmer that spoke of more than just friendship.

Zihua tried to dismiss the uneasy feeling that surged within her. She convinced herself that she must have misinterpreted Wu Jian's gaze, attributing it to her own overactive imagination. After all, she cherished their friendship deeply and had never considered the possibility of anything more. It was easier to believe that she had simply seen things wrongly rather than entertain the idea of a different kind of affection blossoming between them. Determined to maintain their close bond, Zihua pushed aside her doubts and resolved to carry on as if nothing had changed.

As Wu Jian basked in the happiness of their close bond, a sense of unease crept over him. He couldn't help but notice the increasing number of male patients who sought Zihua's attention, attempting to strike up conversations with her. While he trusted her completely, a flicker of concern ignited within him. He wondered if these interactions held deeper intentions and if Zihua was aware of the attention she was receiving. Wanting to protect her from any potential harm, Wu Jian resolved to keep a watchful eye, ready to shield her from unwanted advances.

As time went on, Zihua's radiant beauty and captivating presence attracted numerous followers, both within the village and beyond. While Wu Jian initially treasured their friendship as a precious blessing, he couldn't help but feel a growing torment within his heart. Each admirer that flocked to Zihua's side only intensified his inner turmoil. The once serene and harmonious connection between them now carried a weight of anguish for Wu Jian. He struggled to reconcile his own feelings, torn between the joy of her friendship and the agonizing realization that his love for her had deepened beyond the boundaries of mere companionship.

Driven by his unwavering loyalty and growing concern for their safety, Wu Jian made the decision to learn martial arts. With determination in his eyes, he sought out a skilled master who could train him in self-defense. Day by day, he dedicated himself to rigorous training, honing his techniques and strengthening his body. It was a testament to his devotion to Zihua, his unyielding desire to protect her and their cherished bond. As his skills flourished, Wu Jian became a formidable force, ready to confront any threat that dared to approach their tranquil existence. Zihua observed his progress with a mix of admiration and apprehension.

As time went on, Wu Jian's worries began to weigh heavily on his heart. He knew that their idyllic life together had an expiration date. Zihua, a lady of grace and beauty, would surely attract suitors and eventually be married off. Determined to alter the nature of their relationship before it was too late, Wu Jian started contemplating a plan. He sought solace in the confines of his study, pondering ways to reveal his true feelings to Zihua without jeopardizing their friendship. It was a delicate dance between hope and fear, a battle between longing and practicality. Wu Jian knew that their bond was special, but he also recognized the realities of their society. With a heavy sigh, he resolved to find a way to navigate the uncertain path ahead, for he couldn't bear the thought of losing Zihua, even if it meant risking everything they had.

Chapter 8: "The Unbreakable Bond"

One day, as Zihua and Wu Jian were grinding herbs, a gentle rain started to fall outside. The sound of raindrops on the roof created a soothing atmosphere within their cozy space. With their patient visits put on hold due to the weather, they had the opportunity to focus on their own healing work. The rhythmic motion of the grinding stones echoed in the room, accompanied by the calming patter of raindrops against the window. It was a moment of tranquility, where the world seemed to slow down, allowing Zihua and Wu Jian to appreciate the simplicity of their shared tasks.

As Zihua observed Wu Jian diligently working, a sense of deep respect and admiration filled her heart. Seeing his expertise and dedication, she marveled at his skillful hands and the wisdom that guided his every move. Lately, their efforts had borne fruit, and word of Zihua's healing abilities had spread far and wide, thanks in part to Wu Jian's unwavering support. Together, they had built a practice that touched the lives of many, bringing relief and hope to those in need. Zihua knew that their partnership was invaluable, for Wu Jian's presence and guidance had helped her harness her true potential.

As the rain poured outside, Wu Jian pondered on how to initiate a conversation. Searching for a topic, he turned to Zihua and gently asked about the weather. Though it seemed like a simple inquiry, he hoped it would serve as a gateway to more meaningful dialogue.

Wu Jian: The rain is quite heavy today, isn't it, Zihua?

Zihua: Yes, Shifu.

Wu Jian: By the way, how is that patient we saw last week with the persistent leg pain?

Zihua: She has responded well to the treatment, Shifu. Her pain has significantly reduced, and she is regaining mobility.

Wu Jian: Very good. With your presence, more women in need of healing find their way to our practice. Zihua, besides our practice, is there anything else you aspire to do in this lifetime? Have you ever thought about the possibility of getting married?

Zihua: Shifu, it's a question that has crossed my mind, but the truth is, I don't remember my past. There's a chance that I might already be married or have a family waiting for me. It's a mystery I long to unravel and remember.

Wu Jian couldn't help but ponder the possibility that Zihua might already be married. Though she appeared youthful, perhaps around 17-18 years old, he knew that age alone did not dictate marital status.

At 24 years old, Wu Jian understood the age gap between them. He couldn't help but acknowledge that it might have influenced Zihua's perception of their relationship. The realization pierced him with a mix of sadness and longing. He had fallen deeply in love with her, but he comprehended why she had never regarded him as a potential partner.

Deep in his thoughts, Wu Jian grappled with conflicting emotions—admiration for Zihua's dedication to medicine, yet the pain of knowing that their connection might never blossom into something more. Despite his yearning, he resolved to cherish their friendship and continue supporting her in her pursuits, all the while concealing his unrequited love deep within his heart.

His thoughts were interrupted by his disciple's voice.

Zihua: What about you, Shifu? You're around the age when people usually consider marriage or engagement. Are you engaged?

Wu Jian (pauses, feeling a mix of surprise and curiosity): No, Zihua, I have never been married or engaged. My focus has primarily been on medicine and serving the village. Why do you ask?

Zihua: I just wanted to make sure, Shifu. I value our relationship deeply, and when the time comes when you find someone special, I wouldn't want to interfere with your personal life. I would be willing to move out to ensure your happiness.

Wu Jian: No! I mean... I apologize, Zihua. Love affairs do not interest me. My focus has always been on medicine and serving others.

Zihua: I understand, Shifu. I didn't mean to make you uncomfortable.

Wu Jian: It's not that you made me uncomfortable, Zihua. It's just that my priorities lie elsewhere. Our relationship as shifu and disciple is what matters to me the most.

Zihua's heart swelled with warmth as she heard Wu Jian's words. The sincerity in his voice touched her deeply, and she couldn't help but feel a surge of gratitude for their unique bond.

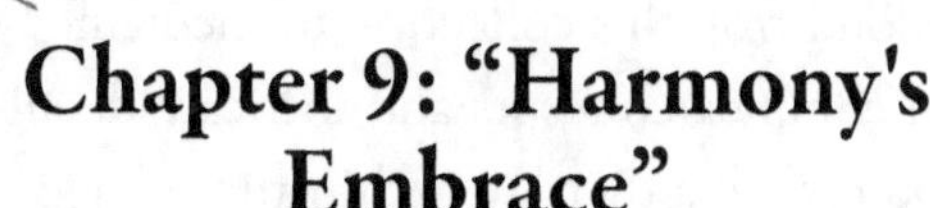

Chapter 9: "Harmony's Embrace"

Wu Jian was relieved to learn that she had no interest in marriage. However, deep down, he couldn't ignore the torment of his own unrequited love for her. He knew that helping her regain her lost memories was a task that lay ahead, but he also realized it was a delicate process that required time and patience.

For now, Wu Jian decided to cherish their present moments and enjoy their life together. He didn't want to rush into anything that might complicate their relationship. The fear of her being already married or engaged lingered in his mind, making him hesitant to change their dynamic.

He resolved to keep his feelings hidden, savoring the beauty of their connection as shifu and disciple. Wu Jian vowed to himself that when the time was right, he would assist Zihua in uncovering her past, hoping it would lead them to a future where their love could truly flourish.

Another year passed, and the harmony in Wu Jian and Zihua's lives only grew stronger. Each day, Zihua eagerly learned new recipes from the villagers, and she took it upon herself to cook breakfast for them both. They had become inseparable companions, venturing into the forest together to collect herbs that would aid their medical practice.

They shared a fondness for rainy weather, as it provided the perfect excuse to stay at home and engage in their herbal pursuits. On those rainy days, Zihua would delightfully prepare various desserts while Wu Jian would prepare the green tea. They would savor these sweet treats and sip their tea, their laughter mingling with the pitter-patter of raindrops against the windowpane.

In the evenings, as the day wound down, Wu Jian would sit beside Zihua and read aloud from his collection of medicine books. Patiently, he would explain complex concepts and intricate details, ensuring that she grasped the knowledge that lay within those pages. Zihua listened attentively, her eyes bright with curiosity and a thirst for understanding.

Their living arrangement had evolved, and now they had two separate beds. It was a conscious choice made by Wu Jian, a reflection of his respect for Zihua and his desire to maintain boundaries. While their bond was strong, he wanted to preserve their relationship as shifu and disciple, protecting the purity of their connection.

Thanks to Zihua's inquisitive nature and unwavering curiosity, Wu Jian's own knowledge and understanding of medicine expanded in ways he had never imagined. Her insightful questions and fresh perspectives challenged him to explore new avenues and delve deeper into the intricacies of the field.

Zihua's thirst for knowledge was contagious, inspiring Wu Jian to further expand his own horizons. He spent hours engrossed in medical texts, researching, and studying, driven by a newfound determination to become an even more skilled and knowledgeable physician.

With Zihua by his side, their shared passion for medicine became a catalyst for growth and self-improvement. They engaged in stimulating discussions, exchanged ideas, and embarked on intellectual journeys together. Wu Jian's heart swelled with gratitude for the impact Zihua had on his life and career.

In the idyllic life shared by Wu Jian and Zihua, happiness prevailed and their days were filled with harmony and contentment. However, their tranquil existence was abruptly disrupted when an unforeseen event unfolded.

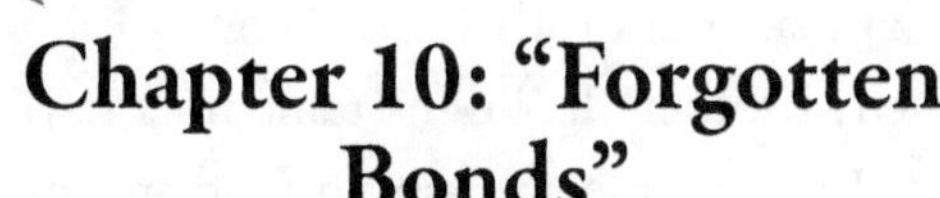

Chapter 10: "Forgotten Bonds"

On an ordinary day, Wu Jian left the shop to attend to a patient, entrusting Zihua to manage their practice alone. Zihua diligently oversaw the tasks in the shop, the scent of herbs permeating the air, as she tended to the needs of their customers. Little did she know that fate had an unexpected encounter in store for her.

In a moment that shattered the tranquil atmosphere, Lin Xia burst through the doors, accompanied by a young gentleman adorned in luxurious garments. Zihua's heart skipped a beat as she noticed the drawn picture of herself in the man's hands. Bewilderment and curiosity danced in her eyes, stirring a mix of anticipation and trepidation within her.

Man: Mimi!

Zihua: (confused) Excuse me, but who are you?

Man: (smiling) Mimi, it's me! Your long-lost brother. I've been searching for you for the past year. It's been so long. What happened to you? How did you end up here?" His voice was filled with concern and a hint of desperation.

Zihua looked at him, her eyes reflecting confusion and uncertainty. She didn't know who he was or how she had arrived in this unfamiliar place. The name he called her, "Mimi," felt foreign yet strangely comforting.

Zihua's heart pounded with caution as she observed the man standing before her, introduced by Lin Xia. Every fiber of her being urged her to be wary, to question his intentions. Though his words were filled with familiarity and concern, she couldn't let herself be swayed so easily. She had learned to be cautious, to protect herself from potential deceptions.

Zihua: (confused) Mimi? Who... who are you?

Man: It's me, Zihua. Your brother, Li Cheng.

Zihua: (puzzled) Brother? I... I don't remember having a brother. I... I lost my memory. I don't remember anything from my past, including having a brother.

Li Cheng's face displayed a mixture of surprise, concern, and sadness. His eyebrows furrowed slightly, and a flicker of disbelief passed through his eyes. His lips tightened, revealing a hint of disappointment, yet he maintained a composed and understanding demeanor. Despite the unexpected response, he remained determined to support and reassure Zihua, masking his emotions with a gentle and reassuring smile.

Li Cheng: It's alright. What matters is that you're alive.

He paused to regain his composure and continued.

Li Cheng: You are Li Mingyi, our parents' beloved daughter. One day, you went to buy clothes for the family, but you never returned. We've been searching for you ever since.

Zihua: I... I don't remember any of this.

Li Cheng: Our father holds a prominent position as a high-ranking minister in the imperial court. He is known for his wisdom, intellect, and diplomatic skills. He plays a crucial role in advising the emperor and shaping the policies of our land.

Zihua: A minister? That's quite impressive. But why don't I remember any of this?

Li Cheng: It appears that you have suffered from amnesia, Mingyi. The details of what happened are still unclear, but our family has been searching for you tirelessly, longing for your safe return.

Zihua: How can I be sure you're telling the truth? Anyone could claim to be my brother.

Li Cheng: I understand your doubt. There is a scar on your right knee, a result of an incident during our childhood. We were playing near the river, and I accidentally caused you to fall. Only you and our family knows about it.

Indeed, nobody else had seen that scar before, and as Zihua reflected on Li Cheng's words, memories of their childhood began to resurface. The image of their playful days together slowly materialized in her mind, and she could vividly recall the incident by the river. With a mixture of surprise and belief, Zihua started to trust Li Cheng's words, realizing that he was indeed her long-lost brother.

Chapter 11: "The Bitter Pain of Parting"

When Wu Jian returned to the shop, he found Zihua in the company of another young man, whom she introduced as her older brother. Zihua and Wu Jian decided to close the shop early, and the three of them made their way home. Zihua prepared several simple yet delicious dishes, while Wu Jian and Zihua's brother engaged in a heartfelt conversation, eager to learn more about Zihua's past. Wu Jian felt a sense of relief and happiness when he discovered that Zihua still lived with her parents, which meant that she was not married.

Although Li Cheng had mixed feelings about his sister living alone with a man, he couldn't help but feel grateful to learn that Wu Jian had taken her in as a disciple. He admired Wu Jian's kindness and dedication to his sister's well-being.

Li Cheng: Thank you, Wu Jian, for taking care of my sister. Your guidance and support have meant a lot to her. I appreciate all that you've done.

Wu Jian: You're welcome. It was my pleasure.

Li Cheng: Wu Jian, it's time for Li Mingyi to return to the capital with me. Please accept this token of gratitude.

[Wu Jian hesitates and gently declines.]

Wu Jian: Li Cheng, your sister is like family to me. I couldn't accept payment for something that comes from the heart.

Zihua (Li Mingyi): Thank you, Shifu. I am grateful for everything you've done for me.

[She takes a deep bow, expressing her gratitude and respect towards her teacher.]

As Li Mingyi expressed her gratitude and prepared to leave with her brother, Wu Jian's heart sank with a sense of sadness and misery. The realization that she was departing filled him with a deep longing and emptiness. His gaze followed her, a mix of sorrow and yearning in his eyes, knowing that their paths were now diverging. Though he understood the reasons for her departure, it didn't alleviate the pain of losing her presence in his daily life. Waves of melancholy washed over him, casting a shadow upon his once vibrant spirit.

After Li Mingyi left with her brother, Lin Xia paid a visit to Wu Jian's house, eager to make salty remarks.

Lin Xia: Well, well, well, Wu Jian. A rich man is searching for Li Mingyi. Quite a scandal, isn't it?

Wu Jian: Let's not jump to conclusions, Lin Xia. Li Cheng is her brother, and their family background doesn't concern us.

Lin Xia: Oh, but it does! Li Mingyi comes from a prestigious family, and her parents would never accept a poor man like you.

Wu Jian: Lin Xia, don't speak nonsense. Our relationship is that of a disciple and a teacher. Backgrounds and wealth are irrelevant when it comes to knowledge and personal growth.

Lin Xia: We'll see, Wu Jian. The world has a way of tearing apart such mismatched connections.

Wu Jian clenched his fists, trying to suppress the anger rising within him. Lin Xia's words had struck a nerve, and deep down, he knew she was right. He couldn't deny the vast difference in their backgrounds and social statuses.

As much as he wished to believe that love transcended such barriers, the reality of their circumstances was hard to ignore. He couldn't help but feel a surge of bitterness at the thought that Li Mingyi's parents would never approve of their relationship, no matter how much they might care for each other.

But alongside the anger, there was also a sense of helplessness. He knew deep down that he couldn't provide the kind of life and security Li Mingyi deserved. He had seen the grandeur of the capital, the opulence and luxury that belonged to families like hers. How could he compete with that?

With a heavy sigh, Wu Jian looked into Lin Xia's eyes. "You may be right, Lin Xia," he admitted reluctantly. "The reality of our differences is hard to ignore. Perhaps it's for the best if we keep our distance."

Lin Xia's smug smile deepened, satisfied with the impact of her words. As Wu Jian watched her leave, a whirlwind of conflicting emotions consumed him. Anger, sadness, and a profound sense of loss battled within his heart. He couldn't shake the feeling that he was letting go of something precious.

In the depths of his soul, Wu Jian silently wished for Li Mingyi's happiness, even if it meant sacrificing his own. The pain of the unrequited love weighed heavily upon him, a burden he would carry in the depths of his being for years to come.

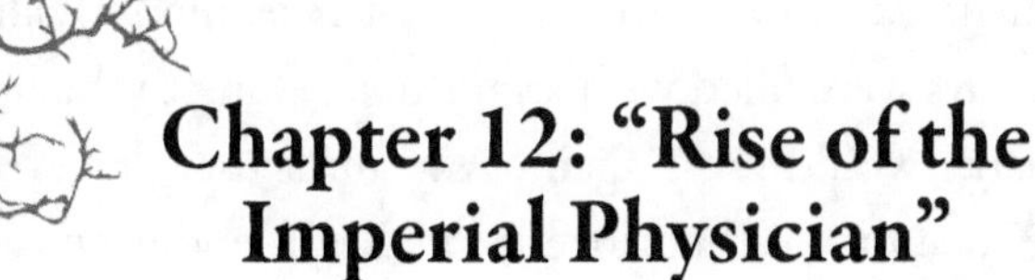

Chapter 12: "Rise of the Imperial Physician"

As Wu Jian tried to live his life without Li Mingyi by his side, the pain in his heart grew unbearable. The knowledge of her true name, the memories they shared, haunted him day and night. In his lonely moments, he would dream of calling her "Mimi" one day, hoping to hear her laughter and see her radiant smile.

The hairpin she left behind became his most cherished possession. It was a tangible connection to her, a symbol of their time together. He would hold it in his hands, tracing the delicate contours of the flower, and his mind would fill with bittersweet memories. It brought him both comfort and torment, a constant reminder of the love he had lost.

His suffering manifested in every aspect of his life. He lost his appetite, his meals becoming tasteless and unappealing. Sleep eluded him, nights spent tossing and turning, his mind consumed by thoughts of her. The passion for medicine that once burned within him dimmed, as his focus waned and his hands trembled. It became increasingly difficult for him to help others, his ability to concentrate shattered by the fragments of his shattered heart.

The weight of his longing felt suffocating, as if he were slowly losing his grip on reality. He questioned his sanity, feeling as if he were teetering on the edge of madness. The world around him became a blur, and he yearned for the day when he could see her again, to gaze into her eyes and feel whole once more.

But deep within the depths of his despair, a flicker of determination emerged. He resolved to transform his pain into strength, to use it as fuel for his ambition. He vowed to become a man worthy of her love, to rise above his limitations and carve a path towards success. Every step he took was driven by the unwavering desire to make their reunion a reality.

Though the days were filled with anguish, he clung to the hope that one day their paths would cross again. And until that day arrived, he would carry the memory of their love in his heart, enduring the agony and pressing forward with unwavering resolve.

After the heart-wrenching separation from Li Mingyi, Wu Jian's anguish fuels a burning determination within him. He sets his sights on becoming an imperial physician, recognizing that such a position would grant him the power and influence needed to reunite with his beloved.

Over the course of three arduous years, Wu Jian tirelessly pursues his dream of becoming an imperial physician. It is a journey filled with trials and hardships, demanding unwavering dedication and perseverance.

During this time, Wu Jian immerses himself in intense study and training, honing his medical skills to perfection. He sacrifices countless hours, pouring his heart and soul into every aspect of his education, determined to stand out among his peers.

He faces rigorous examinations, navigating the intricate maze of imperial medical assessments and competitions. Wu Jian demonstrates his expertise and competes with other aspiring physicians, striving to showcase his exceptional abilities and secure the coveted position he seeks.

With each passing year, Wu Jian gains recognition for his talent and passion. His commitment to excellence is acknowledged by influential figures within the imperial court, opening doors to new opportunities and expanding his network of supporters.

Finally, after three long years of unwavering determination and tireless effort, Wu Jian achieves his goal. He is granted the esteemed title of an imperial physician, an accomplishment that not only elevates his status but also grants him access to the inner circles of power and influence.

As Wu Jian stands before the emperor, adorned with the robes and symbols of his new position, he reflects on the arduous journey that brought him here. The memory of Li Mingyi's gentle smile and unwavering belief in him propels him forward, fuelling his determination to succeed.

With the title of the Imperial Physician, Wu Jian now possesses the power and prestige he once sought. But beneath the surface, his motivation remains rooted in love. He knows that this achievement brings him one step closer to his ultimate goal: to be reunited with Li Mingyi, the woman who captured his heart.

The three years of relentless pursuit have not been in vain. Wu Jian's transformation from a humble village doctor to an esteemed imperial physician symbolizes the depths of his commitment and the lengths he is willing to go for love. The journey has been long and challenging, but he is prepared to face whatever lies ahead in his quest to reclaim the happiness he lost.

Chapter 13:
"Homecoming Bliss"

Li Mingyi sat in the tranquil garden of her parents' mansion, surrounded by blooming flowers and the gentle whisper of the wind. The sun bathed the garden in a warm glow, casting dappled shadows across the pages of the medicinal books she studied intently. With each turn of the page, her knowledge deepened, and her passion for medicine flourished.

The mansion itself was a grand structure, adorned with intricate carvings and elegant architecture. Its sprawling gardens boasted vibrant blossoms and winding pathways, offering a serene retreat from the bustling city outside. The tranquil atmosphere provided the perfect backdrop for Li Mingyi's studies and contemplation.

As the days passed by in the elegant mansion, Li Mingyi's parents began to express their concerns about her future. In the society of that time, being twenty-one years old was considered relatively late for marriage. It was customary for parents to arrange suitable matches for their daughters at a young age. However, Li Mingyi, determined to maintain her independence and pursue her dreams in the field of medicine, felt reluctant to be married off.

In an effort to buy herself more time, Li Mingyi decided to feign illness and continue pretending to have amnesia. Knowing that her parents doted on her, especially after her mysterious disappearance, she believed they would be more inclined to agree with her wishes.

Her parents, worried for their beloved daughter's well-being, readily accepted her claim of continued amnesia and catered to her every need.

They showered her with love and attention, hoping it would aid in her recovery. Li Mingyi's request to delay any talk of marriage was granted without hesitation.

Li Xuan, the mischievous younger brother of Li Mingyi, possessed a knack for pranks that never failed to amuse. That day Li Xuan devised a clever plan to playfully tease their older brother, Li Cheng.

Dressed in the attire of the girl whom Li Cheng had shown interest in, Li Xuan skillfully imitated her gestures and mannerisms. Li Cheng, unaware of the prank, approached the disguised Li Xuan and, mistaking him for his love interest, pulled him into an embrace.

Li Cheng: (angered and embarrassed) Li Xuan, you conniving little imp! How dare you play such a deceitful trick on me! This is beyond acceptable!

Li Xuan: (chuckling mischievously) Oh, Li Cheng, your reaction is priceless! I couldn't resist the temptation to see your face turn crimson with embarrassment.

Li Cheng: (gritting his teeth) You've gone too far this time, Li Xuan. This prank was uncalled for and disrespectful.

Li Xuan: (feigning innocence) Oh, come now, dear brother. It was all in good fun. Don't be so serious.

As Li Cheng was attempting to hit Li Xuan in frustration, the younger brother quickly called out, "Dage (a Chinese term meaning "big brother" and is used to respectfully address an older male sibling or friend)! Please spare me!"

Panicked, Li Xuan quickly ran to Mimi for rescue, pleading, "Mimi, save me! Li Cheng is being mean!"

Mimi couldn't help but laugh at the situation, but seeing her brother's distress, she pleaded with Li Cheng, "Please, let him go just this once."

Relenting slightly, Li Cheng sighed and released Li Xuan from his grip. "Fine, but be careful next time."

As Li Mingyi sat beside her older brother Li Cheng in the tranquil garden, a sense of longing and concern filled her heart. It had been three years since she bid farewell to their village, leaving to pursue her studies and seek knowledge under the guidance of her beloved shifu, Wu Jian. With anticipation in her voice, she turned to Li Cheng and asked, "Gege (a Chinese term meaning "older brother" and is used to respectfully address an older male sibling or friend), have you heard any news of shifu?" "Unfortunately, no news", replied Li Cheng.

Li Mingyi's heart sank. She had returned to the village, bearing rare medicinal books and thoughtful presents, hoping to surprise her shifu and express her gratitude for his teachings. However, upon reaching his house, she was met with emptiness and silence. Distraught, she had turned to the villagers for answers, only to learn that Wu Jian had departed for the capital.

Li Mingyi: Gege, I believe that being in the capital will bring me closer to finding my shifu. There are countless opportunities and resources here. I have faith that one day, our paths will cross again.

Little did Mingyi know that all these years, her Shifu had been silently and attentively keeping track of her every move. From afar, he had been following her news, ensuring her well-being, and waiting for the right time to reveal his presence.

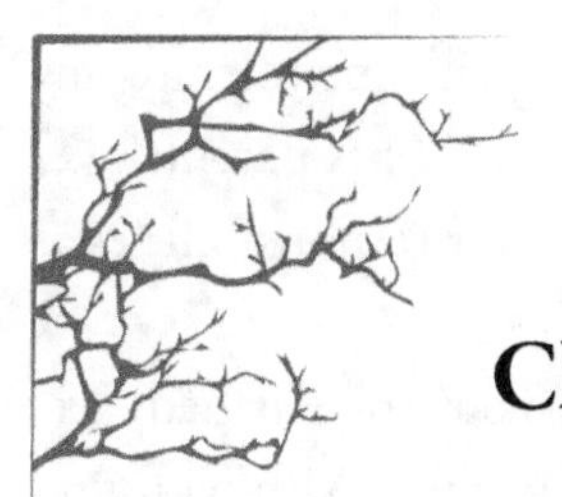

Chapter 14: "Race Against Time"

Li Mingyi hesitated outside her mother's room, a sense of foreboding washing over her. The servant's urgent message had summoned her, leaving her apprehensive about the conversation that awaited. Taking a deep breath, she pushed the door open and entered the room, finding Lady Li seated with a stern expression.

"Mingyi, sit down," her mother said, her voice laced with an unusual firmness. "I have an important matter to discuss with you."

Li Mingyi took a seat, her heart pounding with unease. She knew her mother could be strict, especially when it came to matters of marriage and social status.

"I have been informed that Zhang Xiangyu, the son of a prominent official, has expressed interest in you," Lady Li began, her tone leaving no room for argument. "This is an opportunity we cannot overlook. Marriages in our circles are based on practicality and advantageous alliances. You should not miss such an opportunity".

Mingyi: Mother, I appreciate your intentions, but I must confess that I do not wish to marry Zhang Xiangyu.

Lady Li: Mingyi, you must understand the realities of our world. Marriages in our circles are not always based on love. They are strategic alliances that ensure stability and prosperity.

Mingyi: I understand, Mother, but I believe that marriage should also be a union of hearts. I cannot fathom spending my life with someone I do not love or feel a connection with.

Lady Li: (angrily) That is enough, Mingyi! I will not tolerate any more defiance. I will set a date and invite Zhang Xiangyu's parents over to discuss this alliance. You will obey and accept your responsibilities as a daughter of our family.

Not knowing how to reply, Mingyi's heart sank as she left Lady Li's room. Consumed by a mixture of anger and helplessness, Mingyi found herself trapped in a difficult situation. Despite her seething resentment towards her mother's decision, she knew deep down that she had limited options. Frustration gnawed at her as she realized that there was nothing she could do to change her mother's mind. The weight of her circumstances pressed upon her, leaving her feeling trapped and powerless. As she contemplated her next move, Mingyi grappled with the bitter reality that sometimes, even the strongest will must yield to the unyielding forces of tradition and expectation.

On the same day Wu Jian attended to General Zhang Shuren's health. They had developed a good acquaintance, often engaging in conversations during their sessions. As Wu Jian examined the General's condition, he noticed a slight improvement in his mood.

Wu Jian: General Zhang, I'm glad to see you in better spirits today. Your health seems to be improving.

General Zhang: Ah, Physician Wu, it's good to have you here. Yes, I suppose I'm feeling a bit better. But enough about me. My son's been a source of constant frustration lately.

Wu Jian: I'm sorry to hear that, General. What seems to be the issue?

General Zhang: Well, you see, my son has been in love with a girl he has known for a long time. It's a joyous occasion, but our families haven't been able to agree on the marriage. However, just recently, we've decided to sit down and discuss it further.

Wu Jian: That's wonderful news, General! Love is a precious thing, and when families come together to support it, it brings happiness to all involved. The lady must be very fortunate.

General Zhang: Indeed, she is. Her name is Li Mingyi, a charming and kind-hearted young woman. I've known her family for years. It seems fate has brought our children together.

As Wu Jian heard the name Li Mingyi, his heart sank. He struggled to maintain his composure, his mind flooded with memories and unspoken feelings.

Wu Jian: Li Mingyi... It's a beautiful name. I'm sure she is a remarkable woman.

Inside, Wu Jian battled his conflicted emotions, realizing the profound impact this revelation would have on his own heart. He continued to attend to General Zhang's health, concealing his inner turmoil, but the weight of his unrequited love for Li Mingyi now grew heavier than ever.

As Wu Jian returned home, a sense of urgency washed over him, triggering a panic deep within. The realization that time was slipping away pushed him to make a firm decision. With a resolute mind, he knew he could no longer delay his actions and resolved to take matters into his own hands without further hesitation.

Chapter 15: "The Charmer's Pursuit"

The next day, as their parents delved into the intricacies of a potential marriage alliance, Li Mingyi and Zhang Xiangyu found solace in the serene garden. Zhang Xiangyu's gaze remained fixated on her, his eyes tracing her every movement. It had been seven long years since the moment he first fell in love with her, a memory forever etched in his heart.

Back then, as a young and eager learner of hunting skills, Zhang Xiangyu found himself in pursuit of a wounded rabbit, his arrow having found its mark. In his quest to capture the elusive creature, he stumbled upon a breathtaking sight. There she stood, a vision of compassion and beauty, tending to the injured animal with tender care. It was in that very instant, as he witnessed her worried expression over the plight of a defenseless creature, that his heart was irrevocably captivated.

As Li Mingyi stood in the garden beside Zhang Xiangyu, her heart held a different sentiment. From the moment they first crossed paths, she had not been swayed by his pursuit of hunting or the thrill of the chase. Instead, she condemned the act of taking a life, firm in her belief that true strength was not found in aggression, but in the gentle embrace of kindness and compassion.

For Li Mingyi, the essence of a person lay in their ability to nurture, to heal, and to bring light into the world. She saw beauty in the delicate balance of nature and sought to protect it at all costs. Her soul resonated with the notion that true strength manifested in acts of love, empathy, and the preservation of life.

While Zhang Xiangyu's admiration for her had grown steadily over the years, Li Mingyi remained resolute in her conviction. The path to her heart would not be won through displays of power or dominance, but through the demonstration of a tender heart and a deep respect for all living beings. It would take more than mere words or fleeting glances to bridge the chasm between their opposing views, for Li Mingyi's heart longed for a love that mirrored her own values and cherished the sanctity of life.

While Xiangyu was deeply infatuated with Mingyi, he couldn't help but notice her reserved and distant behavior towards him. Determined to win her affection, he showered her with expensive gifts, hoping to catch her attention. However, Mingyi remained uninterested and unaffected by these lavish presents, not giving them a second glance. Frustrated and hurt, Xiangyu decided to conceal his misery behind a façade of a playful and charming young man, skilled in wooing ladies. He put on a show, attempting to portray himself as carefree and popular. Unfortunately, this only served to worsen Mingyi's aversion towards him. Instead of being attracted to his playfulness, she saw it as insincere and lacking in depth. Xiangyu's desperate attempts to win her over only pushed Mingyi further away, leaving him feeling even more disheartened.

Zhang Xiangyu: Mingming, my dear, are you excited about our engagement? I can already feel the joy and anticipation in the air.

Li Mingyi: (Irritated) Please don't call me that, Mr. Zhang. It's Li Mingyi.

Zhang Xiangyu: (Smirking) Oh, come on, Mingming. It's just a playful nickname. Lighten up a bit.

Li Mingyi: (Coldly) I prefer to be addressed by my proper name. Let's keep things formal.

Zhang Xiangyu: (Feigning innocence). Oh, come now, Mingming. Don't be so serious! Think about the joys of married life, the adventures we'll embark on together.

Li Mingyi: Adventures? I highly doubt that your definition of adventure aligns with mine, Mr. Zhang.

Zhang Xiangyu: (Playfully) Oh, but you'll see, my dear. I have a knack for turning even the simplest moments into exciting escapades. You'll never be bored with me around.

Li Mingyi: (Raises an eyebrow) Is that so? I must admit, your reputation precedes you.

Zhang Xiangyu: (Grinning) Ah, you've heard stories about me, I see. Do not trust the gossip, Mingming. I am not that bad! Though I'm determined to keep you entertained, my dear.

Li Mingyi: Mr. Zhang, I appreciate your efforts, but let's maintain a respectful distance between us. It's important to uphold proper decorum in our interactions.

Li Mingyi has undergone a remarkable transformation over the past three years. Once a timid and fearful girl, she now exudes a newfound confidence and self-assuredness. With the return of her memories, she has gained a deeper understanding of herself and her past, which has fueled her growth. No longer shackled by the uncertainty of her identity, Li Mingyi now embraces her opinions and is unafraid to voice them. However, she remains mindful of the importance of maintaining proper etiquette and conducts herself with grace and tact in all situations. This blend of newfound confidence and refined manners sets her apart, allowing her to navigate social interactions with poise and grace, leaving a lasting impression on those around her.

In the depths of Li Mingyi's memories, she uncovers the truth behind her mysterious disappearance. She recalls a girl from a noble family who harbored a deep jealousy towards her, fueled by her affection for Zhang Xiangyu. This girl, named Liang Xue, was consumed by envy and hatched a sinister plan to eliminate Mingyi from Xiangyu's life. Aware of Mingyi's affinity for nature and her frequent visits to observe animals, Liang Xue began to shadow her, waiting for the perfect opportunity to strike. One fateful day, she cunningly lured Mingyi to a treacherous cliff and pushed her, intending to erase her from existence.

However, fate intervened, and Mingyi's instincts sensed danger. In a desperate bid for self-preservation, she managed to find refuge in safer areas before the fall, dampening the impact and avoiding any fatal injuries. The shock and trauma of the incident triggered a protective mechanism within Mingyi's mind, causing her to forget the harrowing events as a means of shielding herself from the pain and fear.

With her memories restored, Li Mingyi now sees the tangled web of complicated relationships that surround Zhang Xiangyu. The drama and messiness that seemed to follow him wherever he went was something she wanted no part of. Thus, Li Mingyi made the conscious decision to distance herself from Zhang Xiangyu in any way possible.

Chapter 16: "The Fateful Reunion"

To advance his plan, Wu Jian approached his trusted friend Cheng Ming for assistance. They had forged a strong bond when Wu Jian saved Cheng Ming's mother, and now Wu Jian sought Cheng Ming's support in organizing a prestigious banquet in the capital.

Understanding Mingyi's unwavering passion for learning and desire to excel in medicine, Wu Jian instructed Cheng Ming to extend a special invitation to her. He emphasized the event as an opportunity for renowned physicians in the capital to gather, exchange challenging cases, and share their vast experiences. The pretext of professional growth and collaboration would intrigue Mingyi, appealing to her dedication and thirst for knowledge.

To further entice Mingyi's interest in the banquet, Wu Jian instructed Cheng Ming to mention that an esteemed Imperial Physician would be in attendance. This strategic detail was meant to capture Mingyi's attention and emphasize the significance of the event.

As Wu Jian expected, Mingyi's heart raced with excitement as she held the invitation in her hands. The mention of the Imperial Physician's presence at the banquet sent waves of anticipation through her. The enigmatic figure was renowned for his exceptional talents, rumored to have achieved his esteemed position in a remarkably short period.

The Imperial Physician's elusive nature had shrouded him in an aura of mystery, leaving many aspiring physicians longing for a chance to interact with him. Mingyi, too, had harbored the secret wish to learn from and exchange ideas with this highly revered figure in the medical field.

With a sense of gratitude and humility, Mingyi prepared herself for the upcoming event, eagerly anticipating the chance to meet the renowned Imperial Physician and seize the opportunity that had unexpectedly presented itself.

The banquet was held in the grand "Golden Lotus Restaurant," known for its exquisite cuisine and opulent décor that showcased the rich cultural heritage of the capital. The elegant interior was adorned with intricate golden lotus motifs, casting a warm and inviting ambiance.

As Wu Jian anxiously awaited Mingyi's arrival, his heart raced with anticipation. Disguised in simple attire, he blended seamlessly with the crowd, his gaze fixed on the entrance. When Mingyi finally stepped into the restaurant, a rush of emotions surged through him. Admiration and longing intertwined, making his heart skip a beat.

In that moment, Wu Jian couldn't help but feel captivated by her presence. She exuded a grace and beauty that surpassed his every expectation. The anticipation and desire he had harbored for so long intensified as he watched her, appreciating every subtle movement and radiant smile.

The sight of Mingyi's entrance filled him with a mix of joy, nervousness, and a profound sense of connection. It was as if the world around him faded away, leaving only the two of them in that shared moment of fate and possibility.

As the banquet progressed, Wu Jian anxiously watched for the perfect moment. When the time came, he subtly signaled Cheng Ming, who discreetly approached Mingyi from behind and gave her a gentle push. Mingyi stumbled forward, but before she could hit the ground, Wu Jian swiftly moved in, his reflexes honed from years of training. With a swift and graceful movement, he caught Mingyi in his arms, his hands securely supporting her body. The room fell silent as all eyes turned to the unexpected spectacle.

In that instant, as Mingyi found herself wrapped in Wu Jian's strong embrace, a rush of emotions coursed through her. Surprise, gratitude, and a subtle hint of something else. Their proximity felt oddly intimate, their bodies almost intertwined. Wu Jian held her close, ensuring her safety while their eyes locked in a momentary connection. Mingyi's heart raced as she gazed into Wu Jian's eyes, a mixture of awe and curiosity dancing in her own.

The air in the room seemed to crackle with tension, as if time had momentarily frozen. It was a moment that etched itself into their memories.

Mingyi gasped, "Shifu!"

Chapter 17: "Exploring Alternatives"

As Li Mingyi observed her teacher, Wu Jian, she couldn't help but marvel at his transformation. His youthful features had matured, revealing a more refined and distinguished appearance. The lines on his face spoke of wisdom and experience, adding depth to his captivating gaze. His confident demeanor and impeccable sense of style only enhanced his natural charm. Wu Jian had truly blossomed into a striking and attractive figure, drawing the attention of those around him with his magnetic presence making him even more impressive in Mingyi's eyes. She couldn't help but reflect on how fortunate she was to have such an extraordinary teacher.

As Mingyi met Wu Jian's gaze, she sensed a subtle shift, a hint of vulnerability hidden within his usually composed expression. There was something different in his eyes, a touch of longing and unspoken emotion

Wu Jian: It's been a while, Mimi.

As Wu Jian addressed her as "Mimi," Mingyi was taken aback. It was a name he had never called her before, and it sparked a mix of curiosity and intrigue within her. She wondered why he chose that particular nickname now.

Li Mingyi: Yes, Shifu. It has indeed been a while. I never expected to see you here. How have you been?

Wu Jian: Well, my journey has been filled with both challenges and discoveries. I've traveled far and wide, delving deeper into the realms of medicine.

Li Mingyi: Shifu, I have often thought of you during my studies, wondering how you were faring. I didn't expect you to attend this banquet.

Wu Jian: I couldn't resist the opportunity to gather with fellow physicians and learn from their experiences.

Embarrassment flushed through Li Mingyi as she found herself in her teacher's arms, her cheeks turning a rosy shade.

Li Mingyi: Shifu, please let me down.

As Wu Jian reluctantly lowered Li Mingyi to the ground, sadness flickered in his eyes.

At the banquet, Li Mingyi and Wu Jian engaged in lively discussions with other physicians, sharing their knowledge, experiences, and exchanging insights. They showcased their expertise and built connections within the medical community, leaving a lasting impression on their colleagues.

After the banquet, Wu Jian and Li Mingyi decided to continue their evening at a quaint teahouse nestled in a quiet corner of the city. With its soothing ambiance and aromatic teas, it provided the perfect setting for them to catch up on their lives.

Li Mingyi: "Shifu, may I ask where you have been all this time? What have you been doing?"

Wu Jian: (with a playful smile) "Mimi, I have been running a private practice in the capital. Business has been flourishing."

Li Mingyi: (remembering their time together in the village) "I remember how well we worked together back then. I would love to see your practice and perhaps even join you again."

Wu Jian: (invitingly) "You are always welcome. It would be a pleasure to have you work with me again."

Li Mingyi: (sighing) "But it may not be so easy. My parents are determined to marry me off."

Wu Jian: (mysteriously and playfully) "Oh, if that is your worry, Mimi, then fret not. I have a few tricks up my sleeve. You might find that things can take an interesting turn."

Li Mingyi: (blushing and intrigued) "What do you mean, Shifu? Are you suggesting there might be an alternative?"

Wu Jian: (flirtatiously) "Perhaps, my dear Mimi, the universe has its own plans for us. Let's not limit ourselves to the expectations of others.

Li Mingyi's curiosity was piqued, and a mix of anticipation and uncertainty filled her heart.

Chapter 18: "Contrasting Hearts"

When Li Mingyi returned home after meeting her teacher, a mix of emotions flooded her heart. There was a deep sense of joy, however, she couldn't help but notice a subtle shift in his demeanor that caught her off guard.

As they conversed, Li Mingyi detected flirtatious undertones in Wu Jian's voice and the playfulness in his mannerisms. Her cheeks flushed with a hint of embarrassment, and a flutter of uneasiness stirred within her. Yet, she swiftly dismissed those thoughts, knowing that entertaining any romantic notions towards her Shifu would be inappropriate and against their relationship as teacher and student.

She knew that her shifu's role in her life was far more significant than any fleeting feelings between a man and a woman. She cherished their connection and vowed to honor it with unwavering loyalty and respect, keeping their bond firmly rooted in the realm of mentorship and friendship.

Upon returning home, Wu Jian, on the other hand, felt completely different. His heart overflowed with joy from his encounter with Li Mingyi. He couldn't help but be captivated by her transformation into a radiant and alluring woman. Her choice of attire accentuated her beauty, as she adorned herself in elegant garments that showcased her refined taste. Her every movement exuded grace and poise, leaving Wu Jian in awe of her impeccable manners. As she spoke, her voice carried a gentle and melodious quality that resonated deeply within him. Her eyes, with their depth and intensity, seemed to hold a universe of emotions. Wu

Jian found himself drawn to her pink lips, the embodiment of sweetness and allure. But it wasn't just her physical appearance that mesmerized him; it was the aura she exuded, a captivating blend of confidence, wisdom, and compassion. Every aspect of her being seemed to radiate with a newfound magnetism that left him longing for more.

Wu Jian recognized that in order to win Mingyi's affection, he needed to be seen as more than just a figure of authority. Having observed her over the years, he understood her disdain for those in power who exploit the vulnerable. With this knowledge, Wu Jian made a conscious decision not to reveal his position as an Imperial Physician. By keeping this information hidden, he hoped to break the stereotype associated with his role and present himself as a humble and caring individual, rather than someone who holds power over others. Wu Jian believed that by earning her trust and admiration based on his character rather than his title, he would have a genuine chance at winning her heart.

Wu Jian offered Li Mingyi a position at his shop in the capital, and she eagerly accepted. As he looked forward to her joining him, he couldn't help but feel a surge of confidence within him. This time, he resolved not to be the reserved teacher she once knew. No, he would show her a different side of him, one filled with strength, assertiveness, and a touch of playfulness. With a mischievous smile playing on his lips, he anticipated the days to come, eager to embark on this new chapter.

Chapter 19: "The Delicate Dance"

Li Mingyi: Good morning, Shifu. I'm excited to start working here.
Wu Jian: Good morning, Mimi. I'm glad to have you here. I hope you're ready for a new experience.

Li Mingyi: I am. It feels different being in the capital, away from the village.

Wu Jian: Indeed, the city offers new opportunities and challenges. But I believe you'll excel here.

Li Mingyi: Thank you, Shifu. I'll do my best. What will my responsibilities be?

Wu Jian: You'll assist me in managing the shop, attending to customers, and handling herbal preparations.

Li Mingyi: Sounds great! I look forward to it, Shifu.

Unable to contain his eagerness, he decided to seize the moment and proceed with his plan immediately. With a composed demeanor, Wu Jian approached Li Mingyi and informed her that he would teach her the intricacies of the ledger system. He gently guided her to a seat and positioned himself, standing in close proximity. As he began explaining the details, his voice became soft and intimate, his words weaving a tapestry of knowledge. However, as the closeness and intensity of the situation enveloped Li Mingyi, a sense of unease and nervousness crept over her. The proximity of their bodies and the intimacy of his tone stirred conflicting emotions within her, causing her heart to flutter and her thoughts to waver. She found it increasingly challenging to focus on the ledger system, her mind preoccupied by the sudden shift in their dynamics.

Li Mingyi abruptly stood up from her seat, feeling a rush of nervousness coursing through her veins. She cleared her throat, trying to regain her composure, and spoke with a slightly shaky voice.

Mingyi: "Excuse me, Shifu. I just remembered that I need to check on something in the back of the shop. I'll be right back."

Wu Jian watched her intently, his smile widening as he caught a glimpse of her flushed cheeks. He knew that her sudden departure was a result of her growing unease.

Wu Jian: "Of course, take your time, Mingyi. We can continue later."

As she hurried away, Mingyi couldn't help but feel a mix of embarrassment and excitement. Her heart was pounding, and the heat on her face betrayed her inner turmoil. Meanwhile, Wu Jian's confidence soared, fueled by the realization that her blush meant her heart was fluttering. He saw this as a sign of her growing attraction to him, which only fueled his determination to make her his.

With renewed excitement, he whispered to himself, savoring the moment, "Soon, Mingyi, you will be mine."

He knew there was still much work to be done, but he was more confident than ever that their destinies were entwined, and he would stop at nothing to win her over.

For the next week, Wu Jian persisted in his subtle advances, finding ways to casually touch Li Mingyi's hand or brush her hair under the guise of innocent gestures. However, each time he attempted such an action, she would quickly withdraw, creating a barrier that left him questioning his chances of winning her heart. Yet, deep down, he understood that her resistance was not rooted in dislike but in her unwavering respect for him.

He admired Li Mingyi's strong sense of propriety and understood that she was cautious about crossing any boundaries that could jeopardize their teacher-student relationship. Wu Jian knew that his path to winning her affection would require patience and a delicate approach.

With each interaction, Wu Jian made a mental note of her reactions, the way her eyes sparkled or her cheeks flushed ever so slightly. He took solace in those small signs, knowing they were glimpses into the deeper emotions she harbored for him. In his heart, Wu Jian remained resolute.

Chapter 20: "A Sparkling Festival of Lights"

The Lantern Festival was just around the corner, and Wu Jian cleverly suggested that they visit a renowned herbalist together, using it as an opportunity to invite Li Mingyi to a secret meeting spot. He instructed her to wait for him at a quaint teahouse nestled amidst blooming cherry blossom trees. As she arrived at the designated place, her eyes widened in surprise to see Wu Jian standing there, holding a beautifully crafted lantern in his hands.

Dressed in an exquisite ensemble of jade-colored attire, Wu Jian exuded an air of elegance and sophistication. The rich fabric accentuated his refined features and complemented his well-groomed appearance. With a confident stride and a captivating presence, he stood tall, emanating an undeniable charm that caught the attention of those around him.

Li Mingyi, her heart fluttering with suspicion, couldn't help but entertain the thought of what the lantern festival might imply. With a faint blush on her cheeks, she hesitantly spoke up, "Oh, I completely forgot it was the lantern festival. Shall we still visit the herbalist first?" Wu Jian, a playful glimmer in his eyes, quickly replied, "Actually, the herbalist is attending the festival as well. Since we're already here, why not take a leisurely stroll through the lantern-lit streets? It would be a shame to miss out on the festivities." Li Mingyi, torn between curiosity and uncertainty, reluctantly agreed, her mind racing with unanswered questions as they embarked on their enchanting evening together.

As Li Mingyi and Wu Jian wandered through the vibrant lantern festival, they immersed themselves in the joyful atmosphere. They admired the mesmerizing lantern displays, their vibrant colors illuminating the night sky. They joined in the festivities, participating in various activities like guessing riddles written on lanterns.

At one point, amidst the bustling crowd, Li Mingyi stumbled slightly, her balance wavering. In a reflexive gesture, Wu Jian reached out and gently grasped her waist, pulling her closer to him to avoid a potential collision. Time seemed to freeze for a moment as their bodies pressed against each other, their eyes meeting in an unspoken understanding. Li Mingyi's heart skipped a beat.

Throughout the evening, they continued to share lighthearted conversations and playful banter, their laughter blending harmoniously with the festive ambiance. They indulged in delectable street food, savored sweet treats, and even tried their hand at creating their own lanterns. Each moment was filled with a sense of warmth and companionship, as if they were discovering a newfound closeness.

As they stood by the riverside, preparing to release their floating lanterns, Wu Jian turned to Li Mingyi with a mischievous smile. "Mimi, what wish did you make?" he asked, curiosity twinkling in his eyes.

Li Mingyi laughed softly. "I can't tell you, Shifu," she replied playfully. "They say if you reveal your wish, it won't come true."

Wu Jian feigned disappointment but then leaned closer, his voice filled with warmth. "Well, then I'll make a wish for you," he whispered. "I wish for your wish to come true."

A tender smile graced Li Mingyi's lips as she looked at him, her eyes sparkling. "Thank you," she murmured softly.

There was a brief pause, the air thick with anticipation, before Wu Jian mustered the courage to ask the question that had been lingering in his heart. "Mimi, can I court you?" he asked, his voice filled with sincerity.

Li Mingyi's eyes widened in surprise, her heart racing. She paused, her mind filled with a whirlwind of emotions.

Li Mingyi: Shifu, you can't say such things. It's not right to joke about matters of the heart.

Wu Jian: Mingyi, I assure you, I'm not joking. My feelings for you are genuine.

Li Mingyi: But Shifu, I am about to be engaged to Zhang Xiangyu.

Wu Jian: If I could make your engagement with Zhang Xiangyu disappear, would you consider being with me?

Li Mingyi: Shifu, please stop. I have always thought of you as a dear family member, a mentor.

Wu Jian: (jokingly) Well, you know, I've also been thinking of you as a family member for a long time. As my wife, perhaps?

Li Mingyi: (taken aback) Shifu, please! This isn't a matter to joke about.

Unable to process the unexpected turn of events, Li Mingyi excused herself and hastily left, leaving Wu Jian with a mischievous smile on his face. Deep down, he knew that his playful remark had stirred something within her, even if she was not ready to admit it.

Chapter 21: "A Rivalry Unveiled"

The next day, as Wu Jian awaited Li Mingyi's arrival, he received a message from her messenger explaining that she had fallen ill and would be unable to come for the next few days.

As Li Mingyi lay in bed, she couldn't help but reflect on Wu Jian's words and the implications they carried. She admitted to herself that she had, at times, found Wu Jian attractive, especially during their initial encounter before they became student and teacher. In those early days, she had thought of him as a handsome young man. However, her youth, coupled with the confusion brought about by her amnesia, had made her wary of getting involved with anyone.

Once their roles as teacher and student were established, Li Mingyi purposefully suppressed any romantic inklings she might have had, choosing instead to view Wu Jian solely as a role model and mentor. She treasured their deep bond and respected him greatly. Now, with his unexpected proposal to court her, a wave of fear washed over her. She was afraid that his flirtatious behavior stemmed from being influenced by the playful nature of the capital, rather than genuine feelings.

Li Mingyi didn't want to jeopardize the special connection they had developed over time. She believed that Wu Jian's actions might be a result of fleeting temptations that the capital presented, causing him to engage in flirtatious banter with other women. With a heavy heart, she decided to create some distance between them, hoping that time apart would make him realize the value of their existing relationship. She hoped that by avoiding him temporarily, Wu Jian would come to understand the importance of their bond and perhaps stop his playful behavior. Her deepest desire was for things to return to how they were before, where their connection was cherished above all else.

Deep in her thoughts, Li Mingyi was interrupted by a servant announcing that Zhang Xiangyu had come to see her.

Li Mingyi frowned upon hearing the news of Zhang Xiangyu's unexpected visit. She considered it impolite for him to arrive without a chaperone, especially when her parents were not at home. Instructing the servant to inform Zhang Xiangyu to wait in the reception hall, she took a moment to compose herself. She hoped that the presence of servants and the formal setting would help maintain appropriate boundaries during their conversation.

Zhang Xiangyu: Mingming, it's a pleasure to be here. I couldn't resist seeing you today. Li Mingyi: Zhang Xiangyu, why are you calling me Mingming? And why did you come without prior notice?

Zhang Xiangyu: Mingming, I came because we are to be married soon. It's only natural for me to visit.

Li Mingyi: Mr. Zhang, please don't call me Mingming. The engagement has not been finalized, and our parents are still discussing it.

Zhang Xiangyu: Don't worry, Mingming. I will go through the necessary process. It's just a matter of time.

Li Mingyi: It's not just about going through the process, Mr. Zhang.

As they engaged in their conversation, a servant hurriedly entered and announced that a doctor had arrived to check on Li Mingyi. Her heart skipped a beat, realizing that it was her teacher, Wu Jian. Panic coursed through her veins, causing her to falter in her words. She had used the excuse of being sick to justify her absence, never anticipating that her teacher would show up personally. Thoughts raced through her mind. Trying to regain her composure, she exchanged a quick glance with Zhang Xiangyu, hoping he wouldn't suspect anything amiss. She braced herself for the inevitable encounter with her teacher, unsure of how to navigate this delicate situation.

"Invite him in," she instructed the servant.

As Wu Jian entered the room, his gaze fell upon Zhang Xiangyu. Recognition flickered in his eyes, for he had encountered him once before while visiting his father. Wu Jian silently hoped that Zhang Xiangyu wouldn't recognize him. Their previous encounter had been brief, with only a courteous exchange of greetings, and Zhang Xiangyu had left him and his father alone.

Fortunately, Wu Jian had chosen to dress in simple attire rather than his official physician's robes. He blended into the room, appearing like any other visitor.

As Wu Jian walked into the room, surprise quickly morphed into a familiar blend of emotions he knew all too well. In their village, whenever suitors approached Mingyi, he would experience a mix of irritation and anger. Those feelings resurfaced now, reminding him of the competition he faced for her affections. Despite his efforts to remain composed, the presence of two suitors stirred a possessive fire within him.

Chapter 22: "A Rivalry Unveiled"

Wu Jian: I heard that you are unwell, Mingyi, so I came to check on you personally.

Zhang Xiangyu: Mingming, are you sick? And who is this?

Li Mingyi: Oh, it's just a cold, nothing serious. This is my teacher, Wu Jian, also known as the Jade Physician in Qingmei. He has been there for me and helped me a lot.

Zhang Xiangyu: I see. Well, thank you for taking care of our Mingming.

Wu Jian: (irritably) Our? Mr. Zhang, let's not jump to conclusions. Mingyi and I have a teacher-student relationship, and her well-being is my concern.

Li Mingyi: Xiangyu, please behave in front of my shifu.

As Wu Jian heard Li Mingyi address the other guy as "Xiangyu," a slight frown tugged at his brow.

Zhang Xiangyu: (defensively) Our engagement is in the process of being finalized. We are meant to be together, and there should be no difference between Mingming and me.

Wu Jian: (firmly) It's not for you to decide, Mr. Zhang. Now, if you'll excuse us, I would like to have a private conversation with my student and provide her with medical treatment for her cold.

Zhang Xiangyu's disappointment became apparent as he cast a lingering gaze towards Li Mingyi. With a tinge of sadness in his voice, he bid farewell to everyone, his disappointment palpable.

As Zhang Xiangyu departed, Wu Jian motioned for the servants to leave, indicating his desire for a private conversation with his student. Li Mingyi was on the verge of intervening, but the stern gaze from Wu Jian halted her in her tracks. Understanding his unspoken warning, she refrained from speaking further and allowed the space for Wu Jian to address matters in private. The atmosphere became charged with tension as they stood in silence.

Wu Jian's gaze bore into Li Mingyi with a mix of anger and jealousy. His eyes burned with intensity, betraying his inner turmoil as he struggled to contain his emotions. It was a piercing look that spoke volumes, revealing his deep frustration and possessiveness over her.

Li Mingyi's lips parted, ready to inquire about Wu Jian's intentions, but before she could utter a single syllable, Wu Jian lunged towards her. Their mouths met in a passionate kiss, enveloping them both in a whirlwind of unspoken emotions. The intensity of their connection silenced any remaining questions, leaving them lost in the moment.

As the reality of the situation sank in, Li Mingyi instinctively pushed herself away from Wu Jian's grasp, desperately trying to create distance between them. However, he stubbornly clung to her, refusing to let go. She gathered her thoughts, about to utter the words that they couldn't continue like this, that it was wrong. But before she could even form a complete sentence, Wu Jian's voice cut through the air, interrupting her.

"Li Mingyi, how dare you call him 'Xiangyu' in my presence?" Wu Jian's tone dripped with a mix of anger and possessiveness, his eyes narrowing with a jealous glare. His question hung in the air, leaving Li Mingyi momentarily stunned, caught off guard by his sudden outburst.

She struggled to find the right words to explain, her mind racing. The reality of the situation weighed heavily upon her, the conflict between her duty as his student and her growing feelings for him. But in that moment, all she could do was meet Wu Jian's gaze, her own eyes filled with a mix of fear, confusion, and an undeniable sense of something else.

Chapter 23: "A Promise Fulfilled"

Li Mingyi's emotions swirled within her, a mixture of shock and disbelief. The transformation of her once patient and kindhearted teacher into someone so angry and possessive took her by surprise. She had never witnessed this side of him before, and it shattered her preconceived notions of who he was. The stark contrast between his usual demeanor and the intensity in his eyes left her bewildered and unsettled. The realization that he could harbor such strong emotions shook her to the core, and she struggled to reconcile the image of her teacher with the person standing before her in that moment.

Wu Jian's surprise flickered briefly across his face as he pulled away from Li Mingyi. He sternly instructed her to cease all interaction with Zhang Xiangyu and await his forthcoming news. Wu Jian turned and left, leaving Li Mingyi standing there, bewildered and unsure of what had just transpired between them.

Upon returning home, Wu Jian felt a sense of urgency and determination. He resolved that he could wait no longer.

In Wu Jian's heart, the burning desire to marry his beloved fueled his determination to secure a grand reward from the emperor. Aware of the emperor's mother's obsession with a fabled luminous pearl, renowned for its rumored ability to restore youth, he saw an opportunity to fulfill both his love and ambition.

Fortuitously, Wu Jian's vast network of connections led him to Liang Xue, the hidden possessor of the coveted luminous pearl, which had eluded the emperor's mother for an eternity. Wu Jian embarked on a perilous journey to save Liang Xue from impending danger, showcasing his resourcefulness.

In exchange for his valiant efforts, Wu Jian skillfully negotiated with Liang Xue, requesting the luminous pearl as payment. With the pearl now in his possession, he awaited the opportune moment to present it to the emperor's mother, knowing the granting of her long-cherished desire would pave the way for his marriage to his beloved. The anticipation of achieving both his personal happiness and gaining favor with the imperial family coursed through Wu Jian's veins.

The next day, Wu Jian requested an audience with the Empress Dowager and presented her with the luminous pearl. Overwhelmed with joy, the Empress Dowager promised to grant him any wish he desired. Astounded by the opportunity, Wu Jian boldly asked for the ultimate prize – the marriage between him and Li Mingyi, the daughter of Li Guang, Minister of Justice.

The request carried great weight, as it would unite their families and cement their bond. The Empress Dowager, intrigued by his boldness, contemplated the request, realizing the potential benefits it held.

The Empress Dowager was fearful that Li Guang, being a high-ranking minister, would arrange a marriage for his daughter with another influential minister who could potentially pose a threat to the emperor's authority. Wu Jian, though holding a prestigious position, lacked significant political influence, making him an ideal choice. By bestowing the marriage between Wu Jian and Li Mingyi, the Empress Dowager could ensure that her interests were protected, as Wu Jian's limited political clout would minimize the chances of him becoming a political rival. It could be a strategic decision to safeguard the emperor's stability and maintain the balance of power within the court. The Empress Dowager agreed to the proposal.

Wu Jian's heart swelled with a mixture of joy and relief, as he realized that his plan had succeeded and he would have a chance to marry the woman he loved.

Wu Jian: Your Majesty, I am grateful for your previous approval. However, I have one more humble request. I kindly ask for your permission to hold the wedding ceremony between Li Mingyi and me on this Sunday, which marks an auspicious date according to our traditions.

Empress Dowager was initially taken aback by the request for such a swift wedding ceremony, but then a smile curved on her lips.

Empress Dowager: Very well, Wu Jian, I shall grant your request.

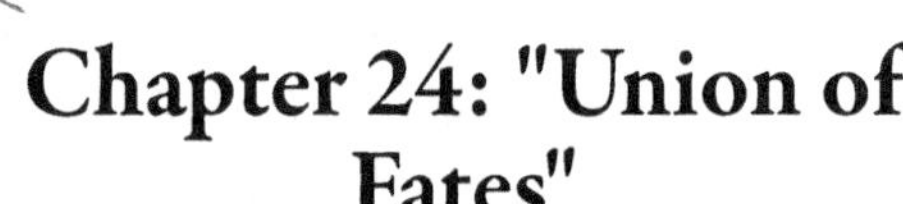

Chapter 24: "Union of Fates"

On the same day, the edict from the Empress Dowager was swiftly delivered to the house of Minister Li Guang. The sealed document bore the official approval for the wedding ceremony between Wu Jian and Li Mingyi.

With cautious anticipation, the residents of Minister Li Guang's house carefully unsealed the edict from the Empress Dowager. To their surprise, it did not mention the name of the Imperial Physician, leaving them puzzled and bewildered. Li Mingyi's father, obliged to accept the edict, embarked on a quest to uncover the identity of the mysterious individual within the court. Meanwhile, Li Mingyi's mother busily attended to the myriad tasks involved in preparing for the upcoming marriage, leaving no stone unturned to ensure a flawless celebration.

As the news of the edict reached Li Mingyi, a wave of frustration and shock washed over her. She couldn't believe that she was being forced to marry a complete stranger.

While Li Mingyi didn't harbor romantic feelings for Zhang Xiangyu, the thought of him being unaware of the situation added another layer of worry. He had left the capital to assist his general father, so he would only discover the news of the wedding after it had already taken place.

However, the person who occupied her thoughts the most was her shifu, Wu Jian. She was deeply concerned about his reaction and feared that he might resort to drastic measures. Their previous encounter had left her shaken, and she couldn't predict how he would handle this unexpected turn of events.

Fearing Wu Jian's reaction, Li Mingyi made the difficult decision to be unfilial and not invite him to the wedding. Instead, she planned to write him a letter of invitation and pretend that the servants failed to deliver it in time due to the haste of the events. She hoped this would soften the blow and avoid any confrontation before the wedding took place.

Escaping was not an option for Li Mingyi, as defying the royal order would bring certain death upon her family. The weight of this realization compelled her to accept her fate and proceed with the marriage to a stranger, knowing that the consequences of refusal were too dire to bear.

On the day of the wedding, Wu Jian felt a wave of nervousness wash over him. He could hardly believe that the moment he had been anticipating and dreading had finally arrived. The reality of the situation was both surreal and overwhelming for him.

On the wedding day, Wu Jian arrived at the bride's house to collect Li Mingyi. He was filled with anticipation as he awaited her arrival. When she emerged, he was awestruck by her beautiful figure. She wore a stunning red wedding dress adorned with intricate embroidery, symbolizing good fortune and joy. A delicate veil covered her face, adding an air of mystery and anticipation. Li Mingyi was gracefully escorted into a palanquin, and Wu Jian, filled with pride, led the way to his home.

Upon reaching their destination, a ceremonial space was prepared. Surrounded by their loved ones, they exchanged three solemn bows, sealing their union in the presence of their ancestors and deities. With each bow, their commitment to each other grew stronger. As they completed the final bow, they were officially proclaimed husband and wife, marking the beginning of their shared journey.

Wu Jian spent the evening attending to the guests. Meanwhile, Li Mingyi patiently waited for him in his room, her heart filled with a mix of fear and nervousness. As the last guest bid their farewells and her parents departed, a sense of heightened tension enveloped Wu Jian. Taking a moment to compose himself, he stood outside the room, taking a deep breath to steady his racing heart before finally entering.

Now was the moment for Wu Jian to gently remove the veil that concealed Li Mingyi's face. As he carefully unveiled her, his eyes widened in awe and astonishment. Li Mingyi stood before him, radiant and enchanting, her features a harmonious blend of grace and elegance. Her eyes, sparkling like stars, held a depth that captivated his soul, while her lips, delicately curved with red color.

Overwhelmed by the sight before him, Wu Jian found himself unable to believe that this enchanting woman was now his bride. It felt like a dream come true after years of arduous effort, inner struggles, and countless hurdles. He had pursued this love with unwavering determination, never faltering in his belief that they were destined to be together.

In that moment, as he gazed into her eyes, Wu Jian's heart swelled with a profound sense of gratitude and joy. The years of longing, sacrifice, and perseverance had finally led him to this extraordinary moment, where he stood before the woman who had captured his heart completely.

Li Mingyi's heart raced with apprehension as she anticipated the unveiling of her groom. The fear of an unknown, potentially terrible match weighed heavily on her. However, as Wu Jian removed her veil, Li Mingyi was utterly shocked by the sight before her, her eyes wide with astonishment.

Numerous questions tumbled in her mind, yearning to be expressed, but the only thing that she exclaimed was: "Shifu!".

End of Part 1